W9-AWH-689

DATE DUE

E
Mon   Moncure, Jane Belk
        My "I" sound box

ENCYCLOPAEDIA BRITANNICA
EDUCATIONAL CORPORATION
310 S. Michigan Avenue   •   Chicago, Illinois 60604

85361

My

Sound Box

by Jane Belk Moncure

illustrated by Linda Sommers

THE CHILD'S WORLD

ELGIN, ILLINOIS 60120

Library of Congress Cataloging in Publication Data

Moncure, Jane Belk.
  My I sound box.

  (Sound box books)
  SUMMARY: A little boy fills his sound box with many
words beginning with the letter "I".
  [1. Alphabet] I. Sommers, Linda. II. Title.
III. Series.
PZ7.M739My1   [E]   78-8373
ISBN 0-89565-045-2

Distributed by Childrens Press, 1224 West Van Buren Street, Chicago,
Illinois 60607.

ⓒ 1978 The Child's World, Inc.

My ''I'' Sound Box

Little  had a box.

"I will find things that begin with my 'l' sound," he said.

"I will put them into my sound  box."

Little   looked under the leaves

and found lizards.

Did he put leaves and lizards into his box?
He did.

Then Little　　　looked behind some

logs

and found　lambs.

They were little lambs.

"You must be lost," said Little   So he put
the little lambs and the logs
into the box with the leaves
and lizards.

Then Little  walked to a

lake.

The lizards leaped out of the box.

But Little  put them back.

"I do not like leaping lizards," he said.

Little looked in the

lake
and found a lobster.

He lifted the lobster into the box . . .
carefully . . .

because the lobster had long pinchers.

Then Little   saw a   lighthouse by the lake.

He went inside the lighthouse.

The ..... lantern was not on.

So Little climbed up the

ladder . . .

and lit the
lantern.

"Someone may be lost," he said.

Little  heard a loud roar.

He opened the door and found a little

lion.

17

The little lion licked him.

The little lion sat in his lap.

He gave the lion
a lollipop.
''You must be lost,''
he said.
''You belong in my
sound box.''

Little  heard another loud roar.

He opened the door

and found a little leopard.

The little leopard
licked him.

The little leopard sat in his lap.

Little

gave the leopard a lollipop.

"You must be lost," he said.

"You belong in my box, too."

But when he put the little leopard into the box . . .

the lobster pinched the leopard's leg.

The leopard leaped; then the lion leaped.

The lamb leaped,

and the

lizards leaped, too.

So Little

put the lobster into
a lobster pot!

Just then he heard another loud roar.

He opened the door and saw

a locomotive.

lobster in lobster pot

logs and ladder

leaves and lizards

leopard licking lollipop

"Let's go for a long ride!" he said.

lion and lambs

locomotive

And they did.

Can you read these words with Little  ?

lamp

letter

lime

lemon

lovebirds

light

ladybug

lace

lettuce

llama

lark

lady

llama

lock

lily

lifeguard

29